D1443270

PENNY DRAWS
A SCHOOL PLAY

ALSO BY SARA SHEPARD

Penny Draws a Best Friend

PENNY DRAWS

A SCHOOL PLAY

SARA SHEPARD

G. P. PUTNAM'S SONS

G. P. PUTNAM'S SONS
An imprint of Penguin Random House LLC, New York

Produced by Alloy Entertainment
30 Hudson Yards, 22nd floor • New York, NY 10001

First published in the United States of America by G. P. Putnam's Sons,
an imprint of Penguin Random House LLC, 2023

Visit us online at PenguinRandomHouse.com.

Library of Congress Cataloging-in-Publication Data
Names: Shepard, Sara, 1977- author.
Title: Penny draws a school play / Sara Shepard.
Description: New York: G. P. Putnam's Sons, 2023. |
Series: The Penny draws series | Summary: Fifth grader Penny,
who doodles to cope with anxiety, is cast in her class play.
Identifiers: LCCN 2022047551 (print) | LCCN 2022047552 (ebook) |
ISBN 9780593616802 (hardcover) | ISBN 9780593616819 (epub)
Subjects: CYAC: Doodles—Fiction. | Diaries—Fiction. | Anxiety—Fiction. |
Theater—Fiction. | Schools—Fiction. | LCGFT: Diary fiction. | Novels.
Classification: LCC PZ7.S54324 Pd 2023 (print) | LCC PZ7.S54324 (ebook) |
DDC [Fic]—dc23
LC record available at https://lccn.loc.gov/2022047551
LC ebook record available at https://lccn.loc.gov/2022047552

Printed in the United States of America

ISBN 9780593616802
1st Printing
LSCC

Design by Marikka Tamura and Suki Boynton • Text set in Decour

*To Michael, the best passerby
a school play ever saw.*

PENNY DRAWS

A SCHOOL PLAY

THE FORTUNE TELLER

Dear Cosmo,

I haven't written too much lately. If I had, my entries would have been mostly about the naughty things you've done, like rolling in mud, barking too much, and stealing food off our plates. Which is bad, I know, but you do make the most adorable gobbling sounds.

As for writing about *myself*? I haven't had to lately. My Feelings Teacher, Mrs. Hines, said I should write in this journal every day, but things were so good that I didn't feel the need. Fall was great. Not a single black cat crossed my path, and I didn't freak out in our town's corn maze.

There was a concerning float at the Harvest Parade, I suppose.

I just didn't understand who that guy was supposed to *be*.

Over the holidays, all my family talked about was how this time next year, there would be two new babies. My mom really *is* pregnant with twins. For a while, I didn't believe she was telling me the truth. But then my parents showed me this.

Over the fall, Mom spent time with other moms who are also pregnant, including Riley Miller's mom. Riley Miller and I are *not* friends. As for my old best friend, Violet Vance—who Riley *stole*—we still aren't friends. But we also aren't really enemies these days, either. We'll sort of say hi in the halls, but it's not like we talk.

Unfortunately, sometimes when the moms hang out, Riley and I are stuck together. It mostly goes like this.

Still, I tried not to let Riley bother me. I was busy with my new friends: Kristian, Rocco, Maria, and Petra. Especially Maria.

movie marathons   ice cream runs   dog walking (at local shelter!)

There were even moments when I wanted to call Maria my *best* friend . . . but I'm not sure. What happened with Violet was so . . . *hard.* Not that I think anything like that will ever happen with Maria, but I don't want to jinx it. I think there's a part of me that's a little scared to call someone my best friend again—at least officially.

Anyway, it's January now. Things had still been great. I had absolutely nothing to worry about.

Until earlier today.

It all started at lunch. We were talking about the fifth-grade play, which is a tradition. Every year, my homeroom teacher, Mrs. Dunphy, is in charge of the drama unit for the whole grade. She chooses the play, sets the auditions, and casts the leads. We hadn't heard anything about the play yet, but we all had thoughts.

We asked Petra what she thought about the play.

I wasn't *too* worried. Mrs. Dunphy would pick a good play that everyone liked, and she knew better than to give *me* a part. I'm pretty anxious about getting up in front of the class. Forget about being onstage.

After that, this kid Luke came over to our table. Luke is in our grade, and he always has some kind of business going.

None of us were surprised that there was a cone as the bonus gift. Luke's parents own a sporting goods store, and he was always trying to get rid of random stuff they didn't want.

We talked Luke into telling our fortunes in exchange for Rocco's leftover cookies. Luke's "fortune teller" was just a folded-paper thingie that we'd made in art class a few days ago. Most of my friends' fortunes were silly . . . but then we got to mine.

And *that*, Cosmo, is why I need to start writing to you again.

MISS KETTLE

Dear Cosmo,

Unexpected surprises? I mean, surprises are bad enough . . . but *unexpected* ones? It's way better to know exactly what's coming. I know you agree. You eat the same kind of dog food out of the same blue plastic dog bowl every day. Mom takes you for a walk at the same time every morning, and you sniff the same pee spots. You even sleep in the same position every night on my bed—which forces me to scrunch up my legs.

What could the fortune mean? I already know about the twins. That was a surprise when I found out, but it isn't an *unexpected* one anymore. So, is something else going to happen? How am I supposed to prepare for it?

Over the weekend, I tried not to worry about the fortune. I mean, Luke wasn't *actually* a psychic. I also saw him on Saturday, and he'd already moved on to selling balloon animals. Well. Sort of.

On the other hand, I've heard those folded-paper fortune thingies NEVER LIE. In second grade, this girl Maddy did one, and her fortune said she was VERY UNLUCKY. After recess that same day, our teacher picked Maddy to sit with the giant stuffed animals during circle time. This was supposed to be a treat, but Maddy was terrified of those animals. We all were.

SPECIAL SNUGGLE CORNER!

So, okay, I was a little bit worried about my fortune. And on Monday morning, when I got to school, I worried it was *coming true.*

When I got into my class, my teacher, Mrs. Dunphy, wasn't there. It was our principal, Mr. Mortion, instead.

Gg Hh Ii Ji Kk Ll

Hello, class. I will be your teacher today.

I've never known what to think about Mr. Mortion. Here's why:

1. He's very serious about everything. For instance, a lot of the male teachers at my school wear funny ties. But even Mr. Mortion's *ties* are serious.

MR. GLENN   MR. HOWDY   MR. MORTION

"Chocolate ice cream."   The Scream.   A stripe.

2. Some kids think he's from outer space because his name—Mr. Mortion—sounds like Mr. *Martian*. Also, someone *swore* they overheard him in in the parking lot talking in an outer space language that sounded like a computer mixed with a squirrel. But I don't know if that's true.

3. Other kids swear they've seen Mr. Mortion at the local indoor pool, getting lessons

from Bertha, this lady in our town who teaches toddlers to swim.

But I don't know if that's true, either.

At the start of the day, Mr. Mortion told us something surprising: Mrs. Dunphy needed emergency hip surgery, so she would be out for the rest of the school year to recover. So we would be getting a new teacher. She was coming that afternoon.

A new teacher? In the fall, I had been disappointed I got Mrs. Dunphy for fifth grade, since she's known as the "strict one." But I like her now. She gets me. She never questions when I say I have to go to Mrs. Hines. She also gave me an A in math last marking period, not because I know all my math facts—I don't—but because she knows I'm trying my best.

For the rest of the day, Mr. Mortion led us through the lessons. Maybe he *is* an alien, because he said everything in the same tone of voice.

Eventually, it was almost time for the last bell. I started to wonder if maybe the new teacher wasn't coming—though maybe that wouldn't be so great, because that might mean we'd be stuck with Mr. Mortion for the rest of the year. And then who'd be the principal?

Just then the door opened, and someone new walked through.

Hand puppets?

This Miss Kettle person seemed completely serious. She went on to say we were going to have so much fun together this year. Actually, she said that more to Puppet Steve. The two of them seemed like best friends.

Then she started talking about how she had a college degree in theater as well as teaching, which made her the perfect person to take over our upcoming drama unit.

THE BOMBSHELL

Dear Cosmo,

When the day was over, I walked home from school with Kristian. He lives a few streets over from me, and we've been walking together for a few months now.

I told him about my new teacher. Kristian has Ms. Letts for homeroom, so this was big news for him.

I also mentioned how Miss Kettle said we all had to be *in* the play. What did that mean? We all had to *speak*? Would we fail the drama unit if we didn't? But I wasn't sure I could get onstage. What if I literally exploded from nervousness? I heard that actually happened to a kid a few towns over.

However, when I got home, I realized that Miss Kettle and the play were the least of my problems.

Things started out okay. My grandma Mimi was waiting on the front porch.

Penny! How's my favorite granddaughter?

For the record, I am Grandma Mimi's *only* granddaughter—for now, anyway. There will be new babies soon. But I'm happy I'm her favorite all the same.

Then Grandma Mimi went through what I call "Grandma Mimi's Grandma Mimi-isms." They're things she says to me every time she comes over.

I asked Grandma Mimi what she was doing at our house. Don't get me wrong, I love when she comes, but it's a random Monday, and she usually has a packed weekday schedule of Grandma Activities—Romance Novel Club, Krochet Korner, and this martial arts class that sounds a little dangerous for a grandma.

Wait, we had to *go* somewhere? That was a red flag. I had a feeling my mom was going to ambush me with a dentist's appointment or a flu shot.

It seemed I had no choice, though. Even stranger, we *all* got in the car—Mimi, Mom, my dad, Juice Box, and me.

Oh, to be carefree like Juice Box.

My dad drove. We wound out of our neighborhood, but we didn't go onto the main road that led

19

to the dentist or the doctor. Instead, we drove into this *other* neighborhood, parked at this random house, and got out. Then Mom looked at Juice Box and me and made an announcement.

I stared. Then I laughed. It was a joke, right? But Mom wasn't laughing with us. She seemed serious. Then she explained that she and Dad had been thinking about getting a bigger house for a while. This past weekend was the first time they actually went looking at houses for sale . . . and, well, they found one they really liked. She also said that she had wanted Juice Box and me to see the house before they made a decision, but all these *other* families wanted the house, too, and they had to say yes or no before someone else bought it instead.

Inside, I was feeling like this.

I couldn't believe this was happening.

Mom wanted to show us around, so we went inside.

The front room *was* bigger, but I liked our old cozy living room, too.

I thought my brother would be freaked out

about moving, but all my parents had to say to him was *this*, and he was on board.

Traitor.

Dad, Juice Box, and Grandma Mimi went outside to pick a good tree. Mom asked that I stay inside so she could take me on a personal tour.

Her voice got more and more high-pitched with every room we visited. I think she could tell I had my doubts, but I could also tell she wanted me to be okay with this. This big . . . unexpected . . . surprise.

See? Those fortune-teller things *never lie*.

Then Mom led me upstairs and said I should walk to the end of the hall, where my new room would be. I guess she thought I might want to have some time alone in there, because she left me to it and went back downstairs.

I pushed open the door. Inside, I saw this.

It was big. And what was that chandelier doing in there? It was pretty, like being in a ballroom. Only . . . did I *want* to be in a ballroom? What if one of the chandelier crystals fell on my head in the night? What if one of them *impaled my eye*?

I went back downstairs. I felt shaky and confused. If all of that wasn't bad enough, Mom took a deep breath and dropped THIS final bomb on me.

THE AUDITIONS

Dear Cosmo,

I hope *you* slept better than I did after the huge news. *I* was up all night, my head swimming with questions. I couldn't believe my parents were doing this. Who can move in a week? Why did we have to move at all?

My mind went to some dark places.

My parents assured me everything would be just fine.

But I wasn't so sure.

I was exhausted by the time I got to school. Luckily, I saw Rocco on the sidewalk—I needed someone to talk to. I told him everything about the shocking news.

I'm glad he understood. See, it was bad enough I had to deal with a new neighborhood and a new house. It was also upsetting that I would be leaving behind all the great memories I made in my old house. On top of all of that, though, I *also* worried about hurting my old house's *feelings*.

Like, what if my old house felt mad that we were moving? What if its new owners were messy or painted its walls hideous colors? I didn't want to be responsible for my old house's horrible new life. I also didn't want my old house to blame me. It was a lot to keep track of!

I wasn't looking forward to the day. We were going to start our drama unit. And Miss Kettle was my teacher instead of Mrs. Dunphy.

In class, Miss Kettle—and her puppet—were bubbling over with excitement. Ms. Letts's and Mr. Glenn's classes were filing into the room and taking seats on the rugs.

When everyone settled in, Miss Kettle called Petra up to the front. That was a surprise.

I was thrilled for Petra. I had no idea she had written a play. Although . . . I kind of figured Petra would write a play about Pokémon—or maybe Bug Man, her secret identity. Also, being the playwright probably meant she wouldn't have to get onstage and speak. *Lucky!* Why hadn't *I* thought about writing a play?

Miss Kettle said we would hold auditions today for the parts with lots of lines. This included the vampire; his best friend, Tyler; his boss at a pizza place; and his love interest,

Clara Sue. Riley immediately raised her hand.

Apparently, Riley took an acting class last year *and* was in a camp production of *The Little Mermaid*. So now she thinks that makes her a total expert.

Everyone got up to audition. Well, those who *wanted* to try out for the big parts—like Maria, who has no trouble speaking in front of people. I stayed in my seat. I felt jittery. Miss Kettle said we *all* had to be in the play. What if she just assigned me a random part? What if I had to *sing*?

Then Violet raised her hand.

Lulu, who's also friends with Riley and Violet, said she'd be an interpretive dancer, too. Part of me wondered if they weren't trying out because they didn't want to be in competition with Riley. Another part of me felt jealous because Petra said that the dancers didn't have any lines. Could I dance, too?

But then I remembered the dance class I took with Violet last year.

Miss Kettle, Puppet Steve, and Petra sat at the front of the classroom for the auditions. I had to hand it to Miss Kettle—every other time we've done a play for school, the teachers chose who'd play which part. It's usually based on which kid is the best behaved, or who's the best reader. This was like a true audition.

People read for the Clara Sue part first. We got a mix of Claras.

In the end, Riley was the one who got cast. Petra shot me an *I'm sorry* look, but *she* was the one who'd have to deal with Riley being difficult, not me.

Then it was time to cast the other characters. Maria got the role of the vampire's boss at the pizza shop. And Luke was cast as Tyler. Finally, it was time to cast the vampire's role. I was surprised that Rocco stood.

Just as they were about to start, Riley got up and walked over to the casting desk *again*.

That didn't seem fair. Riley only wanted Michael McMinnamin because she has a crush on him!

But to my surprise, Miss Kettle said this.

The kids who wanted to be the vampire got up to audition. There was a *huge* line. Of course Michael McMinnamin was first.

A bunch of the boys somehow thought the vampire was good at parkour. During their audition time, they ran around like they were competing in a high-stakes obstacle course.

Some kids pretended to be typical vampires, too, like the ones you see in haunted houses who want to suck your blood. Those vampires just hissed and looked around menacingly.

Rocco was last. He looked nervous to get up in front of the class. So nervous, in fact, that I was worried for him. Rocco was the only one who actually read from Petra's script. When he began to speak, I was confused.

Was that the vampire's part? It didn't seem very . . . vampire-y. But Petra didn't stop him.

So Rocco kept going.

Petra stood up, walked over to Rocco, and told him that he got the part. Rocco looked shocked. Everyone started cheering. Almost everyone.

Finally, Petra came over to me.

Oh no. I was hoping Petra would forget about me.

No lines? Phew.

But then I felt nervous again. I still had to go onstage. I'd still have to . . . *act*.

Maybe I could just be a . . . *sleeping bat* or something?

HIGH DIVE

Dear Cosmo,

Later that morning, it was my regular appointment to see Mrs. Hines. When her door opened, I rushed inside. I could tell Mrs. Hines picked up on my vibe the moment I sat down.

Then I blurted out everything.

I can't remember the last time I was so worked up. And then I *worried* about being so worked up. I thought I wasn't such a worrier anymore. Maybe I hadn't changed at all!

But Mrs. Hines didn't seem to think I was overreacting.

I said I was also so frustrated that nobody warned me about any of these things. Everything was so unexpected! It really *was* just like my fortune. But that didn't make it any easier to deal with.

Then Mrs. Hines had a question.

Out of control? That expression made me think about this one time when my dad let me drive my own go-kart at the fun park instead of taking me in the two-person kart with him. I started to turn the wheel, but I couldn't find the brakes, and I panicked.

If that's what out of control is, I guess I *do* sort of feel like that.

Of course Mrs. Hines had some advice.

I imagined this high board at the pool. I've never even gone near the thing because I'm afraid a kid might slip on the ladder and use my body to break her fall.

I pictured myself trying to be brave and jump off. Problem was, when I looked down, I saw *this* in the water.

I knew there was a reason I hated that pool.

THE MOVE

Dear Cosmo,

All of a sudden, it was moving day. Things were very chaotic at home leading up to it. My parents had different ideas about packing and organizing.

I tried to deal. It wasn't like I had a choice. At least I've been able to talk to my friends about it. They'd never tease me for feeling nervous about stuff. They all saw Mrs. Hines, too—that's how we met—so I knew they'd understand.

Also, Maria made a good point at lunch yesterday.

So I boxed up my stuff, and my bed was disassembled, and I had a bag of essentials I was bringing with me that I didn't want trapped in the moving van and potentially lost forever, but I just didn't feel ready.

Even more unfair? We had to take *you* to the

kennel. Mom said it only made sense with the doors being open so much—they didn't want you to run away. I know you probably don't *mind* the kennel, and this nice woman named Misty picked you up in a doggie limo.

But still. I missed you.

The movers showed up at seven. There were two of them, and they just started grabbing boxes and pieces of furniture left and right in *no particular order*. They stacked boxes of heavy things on top of boxes of delicates. I was pretty sure that by the time we got to the new house we would have no usable dishes and all of our lamps would be in zillions of pieces.

When the movers got to my room, I put my
foot down.

This wasn't good. I tried to tell myself this
was a new adventure that might end up being
fun. I tried to imagine diving off that high board.
But this time all I saw was *this*.

Even worse, the movers were all packed up way earlier than we expected, which meant we had to rush over to the new house to let them in. I really wasn't ready to leave yet. I had a whole goodbye ritual planned for our old house that I was going to perform before we left.

Petal Scattering | Poem Reciting | Trunk Carving

But there was no time for any of it!

My mom hurried me into the car before I could even shed a single forget-me-not petal. Not that I knew where I was going to *get* forget-me-not petals anyway, but that's beside the point. All I could do was stare at my old house as our car pulled away.

I took deep, deep breaths, watching our house get smaller and smaller.

At the new house, the movers were just kind of throwing stuff everywhere again—kitchen stuff in the living room, bathroom stuff in bedrooms. It's a wonder they didn't just leave our furniture on the front lawn.

After the movers left, I noticed my mom lingering in the foyer like she was waiting for a package delivery.

Grandma Anne is Dad's mom, and she was *not* who I needed at that moment. Don't get me wrong, Grandma Anne never tells a lie and she's a way better driver than Grandma Mimi, but she's kind of . . . intense.

But then the door banged open, and there she was.

I couldn't believe my parents were making Grandma Anne watch us on the most momentous day of our lives. Didn't Mom realize Grandma Anne would *not* make the situation better with all her complaints? Didn't she see how *upset* we were?

Well, maybe not Juice Box. He was talking to two boys in the front yard.

How was he so happy? Meanwhile, I was basically hyperventilating into a paper bag.

Grandpa Bob came inside next. Oh *no*. Grandpa Bob has his good qualities, too—he makes really good spaghetti with meatballs and has an awesome belt buckle collection—but whenever he and Grandma Anne are around each other, all they do is bicker, and it's *exhausting*.

After that, the pizza guy came, but Grandma Anne immediately opened the box and started pulling off the cheese and throwing it in the trash. Then she pulled some sort of shaker out of her purse and shook some sort of *stuff* onto the parts of the pizza that were left. *Green* stuff.

There was no way I was eating that pizza. I was probably going to starve.

I needed a break, so I went upstairs to my room. My window had a view of the new driveway. It was different from our old driveway—much longer, with little pebbles. I wasn't sure if I liked it. I missed all the bushes in my old front yard. The porch didn't have a spot where a flag could hang. And we'd forgotten our old mailbox, the one shaped like a dog that kind of looked like you, Cosmo. *How could we have forgotten that?*

I thought about my old house, now totally empty. I wondered what it was thinking about.

I just felt so sad. I'd lived my whole life in my old house. I'd learned all kinds of things while living there: how to tie my shoes, how to ride a bike, and that I was afraid of spiders and clowns.

I wanted to call someone, but I didn't know who. Strangely, I thought I maybe wanted to call *Violet*, even though we hadn't talked for a while. I thought she might get it. She had tons of memories from my old house, too.

Except calling her would be weird, so I didn't. I thought about calling Maria, but then I didn't feel like calling anyone anymore. I felt tears come to my eyes, and I let out a little sniffle.

Then I saw this flash out of the corner of my eye. When I looked out the window again, I saw a figure standing on the grass. Was someone . . . *watching* me?

It was starting to get dark. I felt around for the light switch, but I didn't know where it was in the room. Then I heard a strange noise coming from above.

I ran down the stairs as fast as I could. On the first floor, I turned right instead of left, looking for a door. I went out the first door I saw, a side door that led to the side yard, and then—

LUCKY ROCK

Dear Cosmo,

I stared at the girl I'd bumped into. This must be the person I saw on the lawn.

Even though I thought the same thing, I didn't want to admit it.

Then I realized I had tears on my face. I felt this girl watching me. She was probably going to think I was a huge baby, standing out in my new yard, blubbering.

Even worse, she *asked* me about it.

School pictures? I was glad for the change of subject, anyway. I asked Chloe what she was talking about. Why would I cry about school pictures?

I couldn't believe it. The photographers at our school make *us* do weird poses for pictures, too! They gave us some choices, but they were all awful. The only person who enjoys doing the poses is Riley.

"Sassy" | "Mega Attitude" | "You Talkin' to ME?"

For my school pictures this year, I stood with my arms down at my sides even though the photographer told me it wasn't very "flattering." I didn't care. There was no way I was doing those poses.

Chloe told me she would take me on an unofficial tour of the neighborhood, with stuff that only *kids* knew about. I wasn't so sure. I definitely had to ask my mom.

As it turned out, Chloe's mother is as friendly as Chloe, and she'd already stopped into our new house to say hi.

The moms said that as long as we took a flashlight and phones, we could go on a little walk. Grandma Anne and Grandpa Bob were busy watching Juice Box—and bickering. I think they were happy they had one less kid to look after.

So, off we went.

Normally, when I'm walking with someone I don't know, I get this crawling feeling because I'm never sure what to say. But Chloe didn't let that happen. She pretty much decided to tell me her entire life story.

Chloe showed me some interesting things in the neighborhood, too.

The rocks by the stream looked slippery and uneven, and it was a little hard to see. I thought about telling her that I wasn't really in a rock-jumping mood. I didn't have to do what she asked, I knew. And if Chloe didn't want to be my friend if I said no, then she wasn't worth having as a friend in the first place.

Then again, what was the worst that would happen? I'd fall into the water, get a little cold and wet. Besides, this day was already bad. Falling in a creek wouldn't make it much worse.

So I took a deep breath and gave it a shot.

Chloe started cheering and doing this funny jumping-up-and-down dance like I'd just won the lottery. Then she said something else.

I asked what she meant by special powers. Chloe just smiled mysteriously. Still, I loved that idea. I double-checked that she was sure about giving away her rock. She said it was fine—it was a moving-in present.

The rock was smooth in my palm. I could curl my fingers around it easily. I totally got why it was lucky. Then I thought about how Chloe had seen that I'd been crying in front of my house and hadn't made fun of me. She'd just said something to change the subject. She'd also seen that I was nervous about crossing the stream . . .

and instead of teasing me for being scared, she cheered me on and gave me something when I faced the fear.

I liked Chloe, I realized.

There was a strange look on Chloe's face that I didn't expect when I mentioned Maria. And then she said something I *really* didn't expect. Something that changed . . . *everything*.

DARTBOARDS

Dear Cosmo,

You were so happy when you came back from Camp Barks-a-Bunch. We also got an interesting behavior report.

CAMP BARKS-A-BUNCH
REPORT CARD

Name: COSMO
        LOWRY

Manners: D
Inside Voice (no bark!): F
Plays well with others: C-
Hyperactivity: A
Listens to Commands: D
Shares Toys: D
Eating: A
Affectionate: A+

But I was too distracted to really dwell on it. I was still thinking about my walk with Chloe. I couldn't believe she knew Maria—and that they were sworn enemies! I had tried to tell Chloe that it couldn't be true.

Chloe just sort of shrugged and said it had seemed that way to *her*. And that was that.

Could it be true? I thought about how Paolo beat Maria in the Spelling Bee at our school a few months ago. I couldn't remember Maria and Paolo talking after the Bee. What if I missed how competitive she was? What if Maria is secretly upset with Paolo, too?

What if they're *also* sworn enemies?

But that was silly! Maria doesn't throw darts at pictures of people! Maria is wonderful! In fact, I was sure that Chloe and Maria would be great friends. They were both fun and kind. They both liked dogs. And I liked both of *them*.

Anyway, today was my first day walking to school from the new house. I have to take a whole new route. I'd done some careful planning to make sure I'd get there on time.

You'll be happy to know I made it there just fine. I even got to do the little walk through the woods! The only downside was that Oliver Bracca is also on my route. He sits behind me and hums all day, and now I have to listen to his hums on part of the walk, too.

When I got to school, Maria was waiting.

See? Great minds think alike! Chloe had given me a new house gift, too. Surely if Maria and Chloe just met again, they'd realize that they were both *very cool people* and definitely not sworn enemies.

I wanted to tell Maria about meeting Chloe, but I didn't want to ambush her with news of the girl who beat her in the Spelling Bee and (yikes) made her cry. And what if it upset Maria to hear about me hanging out with Chloe? Maybe I could ease her into it, somehow? Maybe I could pretend I had no *idea* they knew each other from the Spelling Bee world?

But then the bell rang, so I didn't have a chance to bring it up at all.

In class, Miss Kettle and Puppet Steve started right in on play practice. We headed down to the multipurpose room, which has a stage.

Oh *no*. Already? But I hadn't even practiced fluttering yet!

We waited backstage while Miss Kettle and Petra talked about the scenes. Luke, who's playing the vampire's best friend, Tyler, waited with me. As usual, he was trying to sell me something.

I was 99 percent sure that rare coin was an arcade token from Wally Woodchuck World of Wow!

When it was time for Luke's scene, Kristian came up beside me. Petra cast Kristian as the vampire's father, but he only had a few lines at the very end of the play. So, for the rest of the time, Kristian would be the sound engineer. He certainly had lots of equipment and ideas.

I couldn't believe Maria was brave enough to look for Bigfoot with Kristian.

But then something occurred to me. Kristian met Maria before I did. They'd been friends a little longer. Maybe he had some insider information about Maria? Like he *knew* something about Maria and Chloe being sworn enemies?

I started to ask some questions.

I closed my mouth. I had no *idea* what I was talking about.

Then Miss Kettle, Puppet Steve, and Petra called me to the stage. My stomach dropped. I really, really, *really* didn't want to do this.

I felt clumsy and ridiculous. I ran off the stage immediately. Even worse, someone started *laughing*.

Miss Kettle stepped in right away. Or . . . was it Puppet Steve?

We were shocked. None of us had ever heard a teacher—or a puppet—use a student's middle name before.

And . . . *Bootsy*? Riley's middle name is Bootsy? I mean, my real name is Penelope James, so I'm not one to talk, but still!

It seemed Miss Kettle felt a little bad about the outburst.

Miss Kettle made Riley apologize to *me*. Riley mumbled an I'm Sorry, but it didn't make me feel any better. Anyway, she was probably right. I was terrible at fluttering. I had no business being on the stage. I didn't want to do it.

Then Miss Kettle proposed a new exercise— something from her drama school days.

Miss Kettle said it would help us all to loosen up. The idea was to scream very, very loud, for as long as we could.

So that's what we did.

Miss Kettle made us do it again and again until our voices were hoarse. Actually, it was kind of fun. Who knew screaming was so stress relieving? I almost forgot about playing the bat, and Maria and Chloe, and the move, and everything else.

Almost.

SCREECHING AND HAMMERING

Dear Cosmo,

Well, it happened again on the third night in the new house. Actually, it was your *second* night, as you'd been at Camp Barks-a-Bunch when we moved in.

It was late. You slept curled up on my bed as usual. It certainly made me feel a lot less alone in this strange new room.

But then, at about 2:00 a.m., I heard that noise again. It woke me up.

My heart started pounding. I tried to tell myself everything was fine and that maybe it had been part of a dream. But then I heard it again.

I yelled for my parents. They rushed in right away. Well, actually, everyone was still getting used to the new house, so after some confusion and bumping around, they finally opened my door. My mom looked particularly groggy.

I'd just heard the screech! Why had it stopped? Maybe the ghost was playing tricks on me?

Eventually, Dad said that I should try and go back to sleep. The noise was probably just the wind, he said. Or the house "settling," whatever that means. I didn't believe that for a second. I tried to think of various things it might be.

Ghost Family

Rats

They're Coming for Us

The next morning at breakfast, my parents were looking at me kind of funny.

Was he serious? I mean, I'd rather *not* die today, thanks. Because here's the thing: My dad is *terrible* at building stuff. He's an accountant. He works with numbers, not nails.

When my dad came home from work that day, he went straight to the backyard. I was a little bit curious to see what he was actually building out there. He'd hauled a lot of lumber outside, as well as all of his power tools.

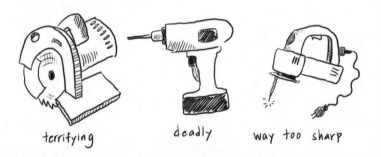

I was surprised to see that there was a platform in the tree. I guessed it would be the base of the house.

Dad told me that we'd be hammering some pieces of wood together to make steps for the tree house. That didn't seem *too* dangerous, so I picked out some good pieces of wood for him to use. As my dad was hammering, he started to talk.

It was true that Mom had been preoccupied. They call it baby brain, I guess. Apparently all a mother's energy is devoted to keeping the baby alive, so she forgets stuff. *Lots* of stuff.

It wasn't *bothering* me, exactly. I mean, sure, Mom hasn't really noticed anything going on in my life lately, and this move was completely outrageous, and I'm still sad about leaving our old house, but I figured Mom would be back to her normal self after the babies were born. I mean, she couldn't be absent-minded *forever*, could she?

Dad picked up another piece of wood and kept going.

Was my dad trying to tell me that I was making up the screechy noise in my room . . . *for attention*? I couldn't believe it.

Except I was pretty sure he *didn't* believe me. Then I started to wonder myself. *Had* I imagined the screeches? Maybe there *wasn't* a ghost or rats or aliens? *Was* the screech all in my head—as a

way of keeping me from liking this house, too?
To keep me from going with the flow and accepting the change?

It seemed like something Mrs. Hines might suggest. And then afterward she'd probably say something about change and diving boards.

I heard an *ow*, breaking me from my thoughts. I looked down. Somehow, my dad had done this.

THE ADVENTURES OF PENNY AND CHLOE

Dear Cosmo,

It seems I'm not the only one not totally sold on the new house. I've never seen you so antsy. You can't find a comfortable place to lie down in any of the new rooms. You aren't sure if you're supposed to be guarding the place or sleeping or spending time inside or outside. You also don't seem comfortable with your new yard or street. The windows have a lot of smudges from you pressing your nose to them. What were you looking for out there? All the old squirrels? Your favorite delivery guy?

I've also noticed you walking into the wrong rooms. As if you think you're walking into my old room at the top of the stairs, but it's my parents' room that's there instead. It happened to me, too. Like this afternoon, I thought I was walking into Juice Box's new room, but instead it was the twins' new nursery.

Juice Box was in there, too. At first I thought Juice Box had *also* gotten confused about where his room was. But then I noticed where he was sitting.

Juice Box didn't notice me in the doorway, so I walked away quietly, not sure if I should let on that I'd seen. I mean, I didn't want to embarrass him. Not that I was sure he *would* be embarrassed. Sometimes it's hard to know with Juice Box.

When I was in the hall, I heard voices downstairs. I peeked down the stairway. Big mistake.

Uh, *no*, I didn't want to show Riley around. I was pretty sure my mom knew that Riley and I weren't friends, but she probably wanted to be polite, and they'd already seen me. Ugh.

I have no idea why Riley thought *I* was responsible for Miss Kettle making us do that scream exercise. I mean—technically?—*Riley* was the one who got us off track, teasing me about fluttering. I could feel my jaw clenching.

Riley kept talking about how we needed to practice the play *a lot*, because all of us needed a ton of work.

There was no way I was letting Riley trick me into saying something mean about my friends. She'd done that before, twisting my words about Kristian, Maria, and Rocco, and it nearly made me lose them forever.

I heard the moms in the kitchen. Then I heard some bleeps and bloops of an app on the iPad. Oh no. They were playing the "What Should My

Baby's Name Be?" quiz my mom had downloaded the other day. The quiz was like fifty questions long—it would take *hours*.

And Riley was *still talking*.

And how are you going to manage playing the bat? Your face got so red when you went onstage!

And you didn't even have any LINES!

Why'd Petra give you such an important part, anyway? It's not FAIR.

She just needed to stop! I didn't even *want* to be the bat!

I needed to escape. If only I could call Kristian's house and tell him I was coming over, but I didn't live that close to him anymore.

What about Chloe? I peeked out the window, and luckily, I saw her on her front porch.

I told Riley I was going to the bathroom. Then I rushed across the street, not caring that my mom would think it was rude that I'd left Riley alone.

Chloe ran back into the house and returned in less than a minute with a giant cardboard box of dress-up clothes.

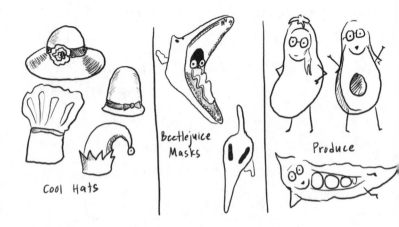

We quickly got to work assembling my disguise. Then Chloe said that *she* should probably go in disguise as well, so she also put on an outfit. In the end, we were probably way more noticeable than we'd been in our normal clothes, and we couldn't stop laughing. We also started talking in British accents. My costume was *sort of* British, but Chloe's wasn't at all. Still, once we got started, we couldn't stop.

Across the street, my front door opened, and Riley stepped out. She spotted Chloe and me and made her typical Riley face. Then she rolled her eyes like she thought we were such babies.

I figured Riley was going to march across the street to make fun of us. According to her, probably, only little kids played dress-up—no matter how fun it was. But to my surprise, Riley lowered her shoulders, went back inside, and slammed the door behind her.

Chloe and I burst into laughter. Best disguise ever.

THE NARRATOR

Dear Cosmo,

I don't know what the heck you ate yesterday, but you had the worst farts all night long. They hung like a stink-bomb cloud in my room. And since I haven't figured out how to open the new windows yet, I just had to SUFFER.

Unfortunately, I had to jump right back into play practice today. But here's a secret, Cosmo: Yesterday, after Riley said all that mean stuff about me being the bat, I decided to prove her wrong.

First I watched some videos to see how bats fly. I have to say, the bats were kind of cute. Not nearly as creepy as I thought. And then I practiced. And practiced.

And you know what? I'm actually good at it! So I was starting to feel a teensy bit less scared. This might not be too bad!

Rocco was excited about being the vampire, too. And clearly he'd *also* been practicing at home.

I wondered if Rocco realized that all the girls were starting to watch him. I'd started to notice that there was a *lot* of giggling whenever he was around, especially when he practiced his scenes.

Unfortunately, Riley was still very full of herself.

Assistants? I guess she meant Lulu and Violet because they reluctantly brought Riley this very fancy pink crystal-encrusted water bottle. But as soon as Riley opened it and took a sip, she made a face.

And then, to my total surprise, Violet looked over at me.

Riley noticed Violet whispering, and I thought her head was going to pop off her neck. We probably should have known better. Then she looked at me with this devious smile.

I had no idea what Riley was talking about. I was the bat. All I did was flutter. I figured she was just being nasty because Violet and I were sort of having a moment.

But then Petra rushed over.

Petra turned to me. She had this strange expression on her face, like she was pretty sure I wasn't going to like what she had to tell me.

But that means *lines*. Lots of lines! There was no way I could do it.

Petra really wanted me to be the bat. The bat was sensitive. Thoughtful. And a little anxious. Just like me. She assured me she meant this in a good way.

This play was so important to her, and I didn't want to let her down. I thought again about diving into scary stuff. But now there was something *new* in the pool.

That's weird.

I turned and took a very, very, VERY deep breath.

Petra gave me the new script with all the bat's narration that she'd written last night. My eyes glazed over at how big the book was.

Luckily, Maria rushed forward.

Great. Now I had something *else* to panic about. Of course I wanted Maria to come over and see my new house. But I hadn't told her about Chloe. And now she would want to *meet* Chloe, and what should I do? They're sworn enemies!

The thing is, Chloe is so much fun—way too fun, I realized, not to share with Maria. And Maria is way too much fun not to share with Chloe. Maybe I just needed them to remeet in a perfect way where they had no *choice* but to like each other.

Only . . . *how*?

THE PLAN

Dear Cosmo,

For the rest of the school day, I brainstormed ideas of perfect ways to get Maria and Chloe together. I think I came up with some winners.

Hot-Air Balloon | Box of Puppies | Perfect Picnic

Of course, some of the ideas weren't going to happen. There was no way I was getting into a hot-air balloon. How do people think floating around in a basket is remotely safe? And I wasn't sure if the dog shelter would let me just *borrow* a box of puppies for the day.

But the picnic idea was something I could actually do. Of course, I'd have to figure out how to get lavender ice cream by tomorrow. I'd also have to persuade Mom to let me use the prettiest blanket in our house, which is made of cashmere. *Only* cashmere would do for this picnic.

But I could totally handle those things.

Thinking about all of this, however—along with the brand-new stress of BEING THE NARRATOR—made me completely space out during class. Miss Kettle has been teaching us regular fifth-grade things besides drama, but I've noticed she isn't a normal teacher. Like today, she decided to mash science and language arts into one confusing lesson.

Miss Kettle seemed to notice I was distracted, because eventually she came over and whispered something. Thankfully, it wasn't in Shakespearean speak.

I was grateful she could tell things were bothering me. I nodded and slipped out of my chair.

When I got to Mrs. Hines's office, I found Kristian in the waiting room. Normally, he plays the peg game—he's really good at it. But today, he had on headphones.

That was terrifying, because Rocco has some pretty big feet.

The door opened, and Mrs. Hines looked from Kristian to me. Kristian said he had a free period and wanted to get the podcast editing done, so I could talk to Mrs. Hines first. So I walked into her office and sat down.

Then I told her about how I was now the narrator in the play. Mrs. Hines said that was very brave of me to take that on. I told her that, actually, I was really hoping for something huge to happen that would cancel the play entirely so I wouldn't have to do it.

PLAGUE OF BUGS

POP-UP TSUNAMI (no one hurt)

RANDOM BRAND-NEW HOLIDAY

Personally, I think there *should* be a national holiday all about fruit.

Next, I told Mrs. Hines about how Chloe said she and Maria were sworn enemies, but that I wanted to change that and have them meet in a perfect way. Mrs. Hines was very interested.

I told her about the picnic. Mrs. Hines seemed to think some of the details were a bit over-the-top—surely I didn't need *twelve* throw pillows, did I? But I insisted that every detail had to be *perfect*, otherwise it wouldn't work and Maria and Chloe wouldn't become instant friends. Twelve throw pillows were very important to the plan.

THE PICNIC

Dear Cosmo,

Today was the day of the Maria and Chloe Picnic. I was so excited. Everything had fallen into place. Mom was so distracted she didn't seem to notice me sneaking the cashmere blanket out of her bedroom *and* taking nearly all the throw pillows off the couches. And my dad was actually able to find lavender ice cream in time!

Clearly, my dad didn't understand how important this was.

I also wrote some cheat sheets for the big meeting. You know, just a few conversation topics, that kind of thing.

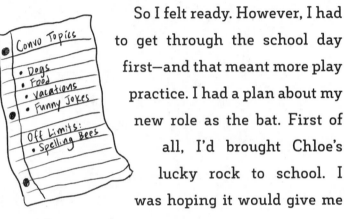

So I felt ready. However, I had to get through the school day first—and that meant more play practice. I had a plan about my new role as the bat. First of all, I'd brought Chloe's lucky rock to school. I was hoping it would give me special anti-anxiety powers.

Then, while Rocco and Riley practiced one of their scenes, I found Luke.

Luke actually had some tips. He told me to breathe in for five counts, hold for three, and breathe out for eight. We tried it together. Instead of saying "one Mississippi," Luke said "one chocolate ice cream cone." Which made me think of this.

After breathing in and out, I did feel a little better—enough to get onstage without shaking all over, anyway. I was even able to read my first few lines.

No surprise, that was from Riley. She claimed she was just trying to help me, but I wasn't so sure. Still, I think all my relaxation tricks worked. It also helped that I only had to read my first scene. Then Petra wanted to rehearse a scene with Riley, Violet, and the other dancers.

As soon as rehearsal was over, I rushed out the school doors and ran home. I needed to get everything ready. Maria said she'd be over after her piano lesson. Before she arrived, I was going to go to Chloe's and tell her that she should come over in a half hour, and that Maria was coming, too, and I was *sure* she'd like her. *Then*, when Maria came, I would tell Maria that Chloe was stopping by, and that I was sure Maria would like *Chloe*. It was a lot, but then they'd both be prepared, and then they'd meet, and we'd eat ice cream and relax on cashmere, and everything would be awesome!

I had just enough time to set up the picnic in the backyard.

In the end, Mom hadn't let me take any throw pillows outside. But it still looked really good.

I was nervous. *So* nervous. I tried to think about what Mrs. Hines said about the anticipation being worse than the actual thing. Surely this would go way better in real life than it was going in my head. And anyway, I'd left nothing to chance. I had my list of conversation topics. I had balloons and ice cream.

I headed over to talk to Chloe. My hands shook as I rang the doorbell. Chloe's mom answered and told me something I didn't expect at *all.*

It wasn't like Chloe would be home soon, either. She was eating *dinner* at her aunt's house.

I couldn't believe it. Why had I not *checked* ahead of time?

A half hour later, Maria came over as planned. And it was . . . great. Of course it was. I love having Maria over. I gave her a tour of the house and my room. We snuggled with you, Cosmo, and we planned to practice lines for the play. Maria was totally delighted by the picnic and the blanket.

I was disappointed, Cosmo, I really was. I was sad my perfect picnic wasn't *quite* so perfect. But at the same time, there was another feeling mixed in there, too.

Relief.

THE AMERICAN CHEESE INCIDENT

Dear Cosmo,

It's been a little while since my last entry, but I've pretty much been learning my narrator lines whenever I can find the time. I had no idea how I was going to remember it all. One idea was to write all the lines on my hand, but the bat had so *many* lines, I'd have to write them on both hands *and* my arms and also both legs.

Or maybe Kristian could be my prompter?

But yesterday, after some thought, Petra decided that I didn't have to memorize my lines after all.

Phew!

I still wanted to practice my lines, though. Maria and I have been rehearsing together a lot. Sometimes, we've rehearsed at lunch. Other times, we've rehearsed over video chat. Which has been . . . *glitchy.*

We never did figure out how Maria's settings got stuck on potato mode. We took a lot of funny pictures, though.

I still haven't had a chance to get Maria and Chloe together or tell them about each other. I thought about it so much that I'd begun to call it Operation Friendship Fix. And this afternoon, I came up with another perfect way for them to meet. Maria's family owns a restaurant that's within walking distance of my new house. Her dad is from Colombia, and her mom is from Italy, and they have a café that serves both types of food. Maria works there after school a lot, and she's super proud of the place.

I asked Chloe to meet me at the candy shop after school today. It's right down the street from the restaurant. My idea was that we'd walk down the candy aisles, and then I'd mention that there's this amazing restaurant down the street, and we should check it out! I figured we'd go in ... and *this* would happen.

Everyone loves flattery, right?

But when I got to the candy store, I looked down the street and saw a big **CLOSED** sign on Maria's restaurant. Apparently, it's closed every Tuesday. How in the world was I supposed to know that?

As I was waiting for Chloe to show up— I figured we could still buy candy—I noticed Violet on the sidewalk. To my surprise, she came over.

I couldn't believe Violet brought up the American Cheese Incident. I figured it was something she'd never want to mention as long as she lived.

See, when we were in third grade, she had to give a report on Betsy Ross. When she got to the front of the classroom, instead of saying that Betsy sewed the American flag, Violet said that she'd sewn the American *cheese*. Kids started laughing. Violet dropped her notes. And then, when she bent over to get them, she farted . . . kind of loud.

Kids roared. Violet ran out of the room. She didn't come back to class for the whole day. The rest of the year, though, people kept saying "American cheese" to her and making tooting sounds.

Huh. Maybe *that's* why Violet didn't try out for a speaking part.

I was about to reassure Violet that the American Cheese Incident wasn't that bad, and that *I* barely remembered it, and probably no one *else* did, either. Not that it's true, but I figured it would be a nice thing to say. But then we heard voices from around the corner.

Violet shot me an apologetic look and scuttled back to Riley. And that was that.

BIGFOOT

Dear Cosmo,

I'm a girl of my word. You know that. Like, when I say I'm going to give you a belly scratch, I give you one!

So when I told Kristian and Rocco I'd help with the Bigfoot podcast after school today, I wanted to keep my promise. The thing was, there was no way I was going into those woods. So I persuaded them to come to *my* house, and maybe I could help with some of the recording there. Kristian seemed confused.

I wasn't lying. I really do have a list of those things. It's quite long.

We all walked to my house. It would have been a great opportunity for Maria to come, too, and for *everyone* to meet Chloe, but I knew for a fact that Chloe has oboe lessons on Wednesdays. Anyway,

Maria wasn't free, either—she was going over some of her lines for the play with Luke and a few other kids in her scenes.

We got to my house. As Rocco was putting down his backpack and Kristian was fiddling with his recording equipment, I noticed this in the kitchen.

It was Juice Box's old high chair from when he was little. He must have dragged it out of the garage, because it was covered in spiderwebs.

We sort of looked at each other for a while.

I helped him out of the high chair before Rocco or Kristian could see. Then Juice Box ran off before I could ask him any more questions about what was going on. Was Juice Box pretending to be a baby? He pretends to be a monster truck, so maybe this is a new character?

Then I took my friends to the tree house. I was shocked by what I saw.

I had no idea how Dad had gotten so much work done on the thing. Surely someone had helped him. Otherwise, it was extremely dangerous that he was up there on that platform without a safety harness.

Dad told us to come up.

I planned on having a stern talking-to with Juice Box about *that*. And even though Kristian and Rocco wanted to go up, I put my foot down.

Then I heard a *hmm* sound above. Dad was staring curiously at something he'd found.

I had a feeling I knew how. *And* who put it there.

We walked into the little wooded area behind my house because Kristian claimed we needed appropriate "forest ambiance." Then we started on the podcast. Kristian said we could record some words and sound effects that would make a good introduction montage.

We said a few more lines about Bigfoot being near.

Then it grew quiet, and I heard a branch snap nearby. A *big* branch.

It was definitely a stick. A *big* stick. What if it was Bigfoot? I mean, Kristian said he lived in *his* woods, but he's Bigfoot! He can go wherever he wants!

I had to get out of there—*fast*.

I crashed through the bushes and back into my yard. My dad stared at me in confusion. But my friends were impressed.

Glad I could help the podcast after all.

OTHER PENNY

Dear Cosmo,

It's down to the wire with the play. I actually think Miss Kettle would *prefer* that we practice rather than learn, because at random times of the school day, this happens.

We were happy about that. Miss Kettle's latest thing was combining a geography lesson with a refresher course on fractions.

She's been really getting the word out about the play, too. I think my mom has received at least six email reminders about the performance. But first, we have to do a dress rehearsal. It's tomorrow.

And today, something occurred to Miss Kettle.

Of all things, she decided the audience would be the *kindergarteners.*

The dress rehearsal will be a tRIAL RUN!

We need an AUDIENCE!

It was a terrible idea. The kindergarteners are loud, fidgety, sticky, and small. Also? They're way too *honest.* In third grade, we did an *Our Beautiful Country* performance. We invited the kindergarteners to the dress rehearsal of *that,* and let me just say they weren't impressed.

On the other hand, if we could get through a *Vampire in the City* dress rehearsal with the kindergarteners, we'd probably be golden. It would certainly make *me* feel better, Cosmo. So I'm banking on it going well.

After school, I was ready for the third big try for Operation Friendship Fix. This one was going to work, I was sure of it. This time, I planned to go to Story Chowder, the local bookstore that sells books *and*—you guessed it—chowder. (And other soups, too.) Both Maria and Chloe like to spell *and* read, so I invited them there at the same time. I picked out a stack of books I knew they'd both love and carefully arranged it on a table. It would for sure spark some meaningful conversation.

The third time was definitely going to be the charm.

But when Maria and I got there, Chloe called my phone. She said she'd made a smart remark to her mom and was grounded for the night.

Admittedly, I was kind of frustrated. I think Maria caught on that something was up.

I started to wonder if maybe the universe didn't *want* Maria and Chloe to meet. Like, maybe there was some sort of important reason? Maybe they were *too* similar—my mom sometimes said that when people were too much alike, they didn't get along. Could *that* be it?

I tried to think if *I'd* get along with someone who was just like me. If I somehow met another Penny, how would that go?

I mean, Other Penny wasn't wrong.

THE REHEARSAL THAT WASN'T

Dear Cosmo,

It was dress rehearsal day. It all came down to this. If we got through this performance, we'd be home free.

I had butterflies all morning. I squeezed Chloe's lucky rock extra hard. Finally, it was time to go down to the multipurpose room to put up the sets—which we'd painted in art class—and get into our costumes.

Someone from the school paper came to take our picture. The kids who had big parts got to take a few extra shots. Some of us were a little more *eager* for photos than others.

Maria's costume was a pizza delivery outfit since she's the vampire's boss at the pizza shop. Luke was the vampire's friend, so he wore normal clothes. Riley wore a frilly dress that looked like it was from prairie days. Violet, Lulu, and this girl Lizzie were the interpretive dancers who represented "the busy city streets." They wore dark dresses that blended in with the background.

Rocco and I had the best costumes by far. Daisy, a girl in our class, had been a bat for Halloween last year, so she brought in her costume for me. Her mother, an actual costume designer, made it. When I put it on, I was surprised at how light and airy—but also sturdy—the fabric was. It almost felt like I could really fly.

Then the kindergarteners started to arrive. That's when I *really* felt nervous.

It seemed like there were even more kindergarteners than I remembered. I know I shouldn't have worried what five-year-olds thought about the play . . . but at the same time, I really wanted them to like it.

Then I heard a familiar voice.

Mrs. Wink is the school's crossing guard, and she takes her job very seriously. I wasn't sure what she was doing at the rehearsal, but before we knew what was happening, she was herding the kindergarteners quickly and quietly to their seats.

Even more surprising, Miss Kettle seemed to know her.

After that, it was time to assemble backstage. But Riley appeared with some . . . *issues.*

Riley launched into this long list of lines she wanted changed. For one scene, she asked that she come in from stage left instead of stage right, all because stage right showed off her "good side."

It went on forever. I looked around for Miss Kettle, certain she or Steve would gently tell Riley to stop being such a diva. But it seemed like Miss Kettle had bigger problems.

I couldn't believe Miss Kettle had lost something that was normally attached to her hand. She was really frantic.

Then Miss Kettle left for the library, leaving us alone with Mrs. Wink. Not that *she* knew what to do. We had no idea if we should just start or what.

The kindergarteners were getting antsy.

And if all that wasn't bad enough? Maria pulled Petra and me aside. She had this weird look on her face.

She took us backstage and pointed to . . .
something. I couldn't believe what it was.

Was Rocco *dead*?

When we got closer, Rocco's eyes were
open. He looked a little groggy . . . but definitely
not dead.

Kristian rushed forward.

Kristian explained that a few days ago, he and Rocco had found a big cardboard box by the dumpster behind the cafeteria, and Rocco had gotten this idea to make it into a vampire's coffin. Rocco liked to lie in it to "get into character." That's what he must have done today. He just fell asleep.

It was clear Rocco was really embarrassed. A few people weren't very nice about that.

Rocco's face turned from pink to bright red. He leapt from the coffin and darted offstage and out the side door.

I ran after him.

He wasn't crying, but he seemed upset. Really upset.

I was surprised Rocco had doubts about his performance as a vampire. He was doing amazingly. And who cared what Riley thought?

I was also surprised he had no idea that all the girls had crushes on him. Hadn't he heard all the giggling and swooning?

But most of all, I was surprised that Rocco thought I *wasn't* going to bomb onstage. He made it sound like I had it all together. From my perspective, I thought *he* had it all together. It was weird how you couldn't tell what was going on in someone's head. And maybe how you couldn't see yourself the way other people saw you.

Then I had an idea.

Rocco seemed cheered up by this. After a while, we went back inside to start the rehearsal.

When we got back, the kindergarteners had moved on to making their own entertainment.

Have I mentioned I hate that baby bumblebee song? Why would you knowingly *pick up a bee*?

At least Miss Kettle was back—and breathing easier.

But then Mrs. Wink had to leave.

When I looked at the clock, the school bell was about to ring. Mrs. Wink had to help kids cross the street so they could safely walk home from school. We'd run out of time! We hadn't even gotten to perform!

Miss Kettle turned to us, realizing our stress.

Oh no. Everything—and everyone—was falling apart. I'd been crossing my fingers this rehearsal would all go well . . . but it didn't go at *all*.

This was a disaster.

NERVOUS NELLIES

Dear Cosmo,

I read somewhere that dogs can sense stuff about their owners. Like there are dogs that sniff for cancer, dogs that alert people with peanut allergies, and I even watched a video on YouTube about this dog who goes shopping for his owner. He carries a basket in his mouth and goes around a fruit market, asking for lemons and stuff.

I'm not sure *you're* smart enough to shop for us—sorry!—but I do think you can tell something's up with Mom. All during her pregnancy, you've been careful around her. And today, you seemed extra alert at every little noise she made.

About an hour after I got home from the Dress Rehearsal That Didn't Happen, Mom admitted to Juice Box and me that she was, indeed, feeling a little "off." Luckily, Dad had just gotten home, too. He suggested that they go to the doctor's office just to check out everything with the babies. This sent me into a panic.

For months, Mom has been talking about her hospital bag. Apparently, when she had

Juice Box, she'd had to go to the hospital so quickly she didn't pack one, and she didn't even have socks.

I decided I'd pack her one. As I was looking through Mom's drawer for comfy T-shirts and looking for her iPad, which I'd specially loaded with soothing playlists, Mom said she doubted the babies were coming. Sometimes pregnant ladies just got aches and pains, that's all.

Fifteen minutes later, Grandma Mimi arrived.

I was *really* glad it wasn't Grandma Anne.

Grandma Mimi said she would be happy to practice my bat lines. She even said she'd read all the other parts so I could just focus on my lines. Juice Box didn't seem to care, either—he was busy with his monster trucks.

Mimi really got into the various roles.

Then we got a call from Dad. Apparently, Mom's aches and pains were a false alarm. The babies weren't coming. *That* was a relief! But they said they were going to go out for coffee, so they'd be home in about an hour. That was fine with me. Grandma Mimi and I were having a great time rehearsing. It was nice out, so we decided to read the rest of our lines on the back porch. Then I heard Chloe's bus pull up. I walked around to the front and asked if she wanted to come over and meet Grandma Mimi. Chloe said yes.

Chloe already told me about the dentist appointment. I was sad Chloe couldn't make it, but, well, dealing with Operation Friendship Fix *and* being the bat at the same time might be kind of a lot!

I also said that my mom would likely take a video of the whole thing, so she could watch it later. Then again, maybe I wouldn't *want* her to watch it. What if the actual performance went as badly as the Rehearsal That Wasn't?

And then I felt nervous all over again.

So we started to rehearse the lines. Chloe loved the play, just like I knew she would. When we were about halfway through, I started noticing something weird happening in the bushes near the tree house.

The bushes shook harder. My heart started to pound. Was this related to the screech I somehow heard in my bedroom? Or . . . oh no. *Oh no.* Was it Bigfoot? I *knew* I'd heard a scary crack!

I was ready to curl up into a ball. Maybe Bigfoot wouldn't want to eat me that way. But then the bushes parted. I couldn't believe who stepped out.

Riley came toward us. I was confused why she was even here. It would have been kind of a long walk.

Then I noticed what was in her hand.

Uh-oh. Clearly, Chloe didn't know you should never, *ever* insult Riley. And clearly, Riley thought being called *nervous* was an insult.

I couldn't believe it. Was Riley panicking? Maybe that's why she'd come with her script. Maybe she wanted to practice. I almost felt bad for Riley. Did she even have anyone else to practice with? What about Violet or Lulu?

Of course I knew what to do! I quickly ran through all the things I do when I'm nervous— the things that Mrs. Hines taught me. Deep breathing, like Luke showed me, and visualization, and looking around the room and naming five things I can see, four things I can touch, and so on. Riley didn't really want to hear any of it, but before she left, she did turn back and say this.

What was next, Cosmo? Were dogs going to fly?

THE PLAY

Dear Cosmo,

On the morning of the play, the first thing I did was look out my window. To my great disappointment, there wasn't a tornado brewing. Or a hurricane. Or any other natural disaster. I hadn't gotten a news alert that the school had burned down—with no one in it, of course—or that it was infested with termites and we would have the rest of the year off.

So I guess the play was happening. Whether I was ready or not.

But I also woke up realizing something. No, it wasn't that Juice Box was looking at diapers, though that happened, too.

I kept thinking about how Riley admitted she was nervous yesterday. She didn't want to, that's for sure. I bet she was kicking herself for saying it, especially to me.

But she *did*. She told me. She was honest.

And I needed to be honest, too. I needed to just *tell* Maria about Chloe.

I tried calling Maria's house. No one answered. I tried her on our video chat app. Maria didn't answer that, either.

Then I looked at the clock. It was almost noon, and the play started at one. I had to get going.

Mom dropped me off, saying she'd go home

and pick up Dad and Juice Box to bring them at curtain time.

I walked into school. I was nervous. *Really* nervous. What if it all went wrong? What if I got onstage and froze? What if Petra was disappointed by our performances? What if Rocco was in that coffin again, asleep?

Luckily, I saw him the moment I got into school.

In the multipurpose room, everyone was getting the sets ready.

Violet and Lulu were practicing their dances. Luke was saying his lines into the mirror. I saw Riley, too. She glared at me like I'd better not *dare* say anything . . . so I didn't.

Finally, I found Maria talking to Kristian by the soundboard. I took a deep breath. I needed to tell her. It was time. It would be okay. Or, well, I hoped it would.

I said that was fine. I could tell Maria after the play, I figured.

The audience was arriving, and I didn't even have my bat costume on yet! I hurried backstage and put it on. Rocco had changed into his vampire costume, too. And he was dealing with his many admirers.

I thought actors typically got flowers at the *end* of the performance, but Rocco didn't seem to mind.

I heard people taking their seats. My heart started to pound. I had the very first lines in the play. I had to speak to all those people *soon*. I looked around for Chloe's lucky rock. But then I realized: I hadn't brought it. I'd left it at home.

Suddenly, I couldn't even remember what my first lines *were*. And when I looked down at the script, I saw this.

VAMPIRE IN THE CITY

Act One, Scene One
Dark stage. THE BAT steps out to the microphone.

BAT: My whole life, I've been a bat. I was happy to bluh bluh blubby blubby bloh blobby bloopy bloh bloh bloo bluh bubble bobyle bibble babble bxnk rxnz bzlkpo

Bloopy blubby bloh bloo? *That* wasn't right. Wait a minute. In my panic, had I lost the ability to read?

I wasn't sure I could do this. Maybe someone else could fill in as the bat instead.

Then I felt a hand on my arm.

There was part of me that really, *really* wanted to tell Petra that I'd changed my mind. But I knew she really wanted *me* to be the bat. So I took a deep breath. When I looked at the script again, the words made sense. I could read. I could do this, even without the lucky rock.

Miss Kettle and the other fifth-grade teachers got everyone into their places. I noticed Mrs. Wink climb into this little room at the back of the auditorium so she could work the lights. Before I knew what was happening, the lights went dim, and the audience grew quiet. Kristian, who was in charge of the sound except for a few lines at the end of the play, pressed a button to start the audio montage he'd created: a mix of wind, city noises, and spooky music.

When I push THIS button, it's a THUNDER sound. And that's your cue!

I heard a clap of thunder. Petra nodded at me. It was time to go. I looked down at my hands. They weren't shaking. I could read the words.

So I walked out. There were a *lot* of people. In the darkness of the audience, all I could see were eyeballs. And then . . . I started.

My voice cracked a little, and the microphone did this screechy feedback thing, but after that, I actually did okay!

As a matter of fact, everything started to move really quickly. Riley did her first scene as Clara Sue, and then Rocco appeared, having suddenly made the huge transformation from bat to vampire.

Even Riley commented on how *vampire-y* he was.

Then it was time for Violet and Lulu's dance routine to symbolize the busy city. Then we got into the plot of the play, where the vampire makes new friends and tries to live his life as a vampire and not a bat. Maria did a great job as his boss. Luke did a great job as his friend. Even Riley was a good Clara Sue.

I could feel myself relaxing just a tiny, tiny bit. In other words, I wasn't quite as sweaty. My script didn't shake quite as badly in my hands. There were a few moments where I dared to look out into the audience. But that didn't really work for me.

And then it was the last scene. Kristian played the vampire's dad, and he said his lines in a booming voice from behind the curtain. He said his first line like Darth Vader, which made a lot of people laugh.

And then Rocco changed into me, the bat, and I fluttered off the stage into darkness. And then it was done! It was weird, but I almost felt *sad* the play was over. I mean, not entirely, because I still felt like I was going to throw up and was very convinced that I was going to lose the ability to read again, but it wasn't nearly as bad as I thought it was going to be.

As soon as I left the stage, the crowd started applauding. We all came back to take a bow.

Rocco got a huge round of applause. But the biggest applause went to Petra, who Miss Kettle pushed to the front of the stage in a bossy way.

Backstage, we were all giddy with relief. I think everyone was sort of in a dreamy, happy state, and some interesting things happened.

It felt like my whole class was friends. For a few minutes, there weren't any cliques, there wasn't any nastiness. We'd all gone through this thing together, and despite being totally un-organized and not even having a dress rehearsal, we'd done a great performance.

All the parents were waiting for us in the lobby. Mom and Dad had flowers for me, and they also had a huge surprise.

Mom said she'd order us pizzas, and we'd hang out in the backyard of the new house. It sounded great!

When I asked around, everyone else seemed excited.

We all headed to our cars, and I was feeling really great. I'd done it! I was the bat! And now we were having a party!

But then my mom turned around and told me *this*.

OUT OF CONTROL

Dear Cosmo,

I was shocked by what my mom just told me. She said she ran into Chloe's mom before they headed to the play and that Chloe would be back from the dentist right about the time the party would start. She was so happy she could make it.

I mean, of course I wanted Chloe there. She was my friend. But I hadn't had a chance to tell Chloe about Maria or Maria about Chloe. But now Maria and Chloe were going to *see each other* . . . and it wasn't in the way I'd planned at *all*.

At home, Dad got to work setting up tables and getting out snacks. Almost immediately, cars started pulling up to our house. I knew I needed to see who was arriving, but I realized there was something *else* I needed to make sure of first.

I couldn't risk anyone going up *there*.

People had to start parking way down the street because so many guests were coming to the party. One of them was Maria's family; I saw her, her sister, and her parents climbing out. And out of the corner of my eye, I noticed Chloe heading to my house from across the street. This wasn't good. I needed to make sure they didn't show up on the porch at the same time without me preparing them first.

I rushed over to Chloe.

I didn't really have a plan, exactly—only to stall her. I hurried Chloe around to the side yard, trying to make it seem that what I wanted to show her was very important.

I mean, it's not like I could blame Chloe. The cactus wasn't that interesting. The party was inside.

But then, to my horror, *this* happened.

I told Chloe I'd be right back—I was going to bring some friends out to meet her. Then I flew into the house and looked around. My kitchen was packed. Finally, I spotted Maria with Kristian and the others by some bowls of chips. Here was my chance.

Except then Miss Kettle showed up.

I was surprised Miss Kettle was so stressed about it. She seemed so cool and collected during the play! And I couldn't believe I was giving Miss Kettle advice. But also . . . I *got* it. I certainly had the What-Ifs every day of my life.

But then I realized—I was talking to Miss Kettle instead of dealing with my Chloe and Maria issue. I turned around.

Where had she gone?

My heart started to pound.

I headed toward Maria. The room had become even more crowded.

And then . . .

I paused, concerned. Rocco and I had promised we'd stick together. But when I looked up,

Maria was on the move. So I told Rocco I'd be right back, I *promised*. Rocco looked a little hurt, but I just needed to get this over with.

Except when I took another few steps, I heard a loud voice to my left. A *familiar* voice.

Oh no. I couldn't stick Petra with Grandma Anne and her vitamin talk! But then I looked down the hall. Maria was turning to leave!

I shot Petra an apologetic smile and told her, too, that I'd be back in a second. Now I had a *line* of people who needed me. And then I noticed one more: Mrs. Hines, who I didn't even know had been invited.

Oh no! I'd blocked off the tree house, but I hadn't blocked off the woods. Kristian couldn't go into the woods! What if Bigfoot *was* there?

I told his mom that maybe she should go find him, making up an excuse that there was a lot of poison ivy in the woods. I didn't want to totally freak her out about Bigfoot. But then I felt worse. Maybe I should have gone with her? Was it right that I'd sent someone else into the woods if Bigfoot was there? What would a good friend do? My brain felt scrambled. I needed to find Maria. Then I could help everyone else.

But it was about to get even worse, Cosmo. Because I saw *this* out the side window.

I could see it unfolding. I knew exactly what was going to happen. And I knew that I should rush forward and try to explain—or try to smooth it out, somehow. I racked my brain for the conversation topics for Maria and Chloe that I'd carefully planned out, but I couldn't think of a single one.

Even worse, when I looked around for a friend to rely on, I wasn't sure who I could talk to. Grandma Anne had Petra trapped. Bigfoot was probably eating Kristian. And Rocco! I'd sort of abandoned him—and for what? But I didn't see him, either. And you know who *else* was missing? Mrs. Hines, who might have been able to help me!

Everything felt terrible all of a sudden. So I did what made the most sense.

I ran.

ALL ALONE

Dear Cosmo,

I thought about going up into my bedroom, but I really just wanted out of the house entirely. So I fled into the backyard. There were some people out there, though, and I really didn't want to be around anyone. I wanted to hide.

Then I realized one place I could go. One place *no one* would look.

It was a risk, of course. But I pushed aside the caution tape and carefully climbed up the tree house's wooden steps. To my surprise, they held my weight. Soon enough, I was through the little door and looking into the tree house itself.

The tree house smelled nice, like freshly cut wood. It didn't even sway precariously. So I sat down.

I felt so awful. Surely, by now,

Maria and Chloe had met, realized who each other was, and relived the whole awful Spelling Bee experience. Surely, they'd decided that they were still sworn enemies, and they were probably both mad at me for not telling them exactly what was going on. Chloe was becoming a friend, but I didn't tell Maria about her—and Maria trusted me. Chloe had told me she was Maria's enemy, and I should have been honest with *her*, too.

I'd probably lost both my friends. Remember the thing Maria had said to me a while ago at lunch? About how not *everything* was going to change in my life? That I still had my friends?

Maybe that wasn't true anymore.

Tears filled my eyes. I looked around for something in the tree house to wipe my face with. As I was looking, I noticed something out the window. More people had come onto the lawn—that's where Mom was setting out the pizzas. I saw Petra, Miss Kettle, Grandma Anne, and Rocco. And then I saw two other people. Two people I didn't expect to be together.

I leaned forward. Maria and Chloe looked . . . *happy*? Not furious that they were both at the same party. Or bitter about the Spelling Bee or annoyed that they shared the same friend. And they certainly didn't look like sworn enemies.

Maybe it was . . . okay? Maybe some sort of miracle had occurred? I had to see what was going on. But as I got up to leave, *this* happened.

My costume had gotten stuck on a huge nail. And now there was a rip in my dress . . . a rip so big that my underwear was showing.

Well, that settled it. I was staying up there for the rest of my life.

SEARCH PARTY

Dear Cosmo,

Why, why, *why* did I think going into the tree house was a good idea? Okay, maybe the thing hasn't crashed to the ground yet. And maybe I didn't get a splinter the size of my thumb. But getting caught on a random nail my dad hadn't properly hammered in all the way and suddenly having a ripped costume was JUST AS BAD. Let me repeat: *My underwear was showing.*

I stared down at the party. Maria and Chloe seemed to be having fun together. They were laughing about something. I wished I knew what it was. I wished I was *down there*, right then, but there was no way I was calling attention to myself. I could just imagine how *that* would go.

Then I heard *this* coming from the yard.

Oh no. They were looking for me. I tried to call out.

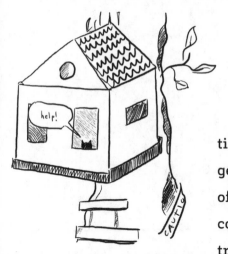

But no one heard. I'd done such a good job with my caution tape and danger signs that none of the guests were coming close to the tree house.

More people called for me. I spotted Mom by the pizzas, looking worried. I didn't want to worry her. Stress wasn't good for the babies.

So there was only one thing to do: pull away from the nail, rip my clothes more, and face eternal humiliation. Except when I tried to, no matter how hard I yanked, my bat costume stayed put. It was stuck. If I wanted to get free, someone was going to have to come here and help me, preferably with a pair of scissors. And a change of clothes.

My heart started to pound. I really *was* stuck up here forever . . . or at least until my dad decided to work on the tree house again.

But then I heard a voice close by.

Juice Box?

I shifted around as best I could to get a view of the person Juice Box was with. And when I saw who it was, my jaw dropped onto the floor.

Riley and my brother, having a conversation about new babies? I hadn't even thought about how Riley might feel about her mom having a new baby. It wasn't like we ever talked about it.

I realized something. They were standing beneath the tree house—close enough to hear me! Here was my chance! But . . . could I risk it? This was Riley we were talking about. What if she laughed at me? What if she immediately told everyone at the party?

But I had to do *something*.

Juice Box and Riley climbed into the tree house to take a look.

Riley seemed totally delighted. I could tell she wanted to spread it around the entire school, just like I feared. But then, for some reason, she clamped her mouth closed and rolled her eyes.

They found some scissors in Dad's tool chest. I was sad to lose a chunk of the fabric, and I felt bad because I'd ripped Daisy's bat costume, but at least I was free. I bent my knees to make sure my legs still worked. It felt like I had been stuck up here for *hours*. Juice Box climbed back down the ladder, rummaged through a bush, and pulled out an old baby blanket he'd stashed there. He said I could use it to cover up the rip at the back of the costume.

I figured it might be a good opportunity to finally talk to him about all that baby stuff. So I asked him after Riley climbed down the ladder.

I also added that I was pretty sure Dad had bought at least ten monster trucks to give him as a present "from the babies" after they were born. It's what happened to me when *he* was born, in fact. Except in my case, I got a bunch of stuffed animals.

Juice Box looked thrilled. He even said that maybe babies weren't so dumb after all.

When we climbed back down, Mom came rushing toward me.

At least *someone* agrees with me.

After I changed out of my ripped costume and back into my normal clothes, I found Maria, Chloe, and my other friends. I took a deep breath and turned to Maria and Chloe first.

Maria and Chloe explained that they were both fierce competitors on the Spelling Bee circuit. Their goal is always to beat the other one in the Bee. And yes, Maria often got upset and cried at Bees. Sometimes Chloe did, too. But despite all that, they also respected each other.

Huh. As I recall, that was a topic I wanted to *avoid* on my Chloe and Maria conversation list. Who would have thought?

Maria asked why we all hadn't hung out yet. I explained that I'd *tried*. I went through the picnic plans, and showing up at her parents' restaurant, and making that big stack of books at the bookstore. I even talked about the other ideas I had— the boxes of puppies, the hot-air balloon ride.

Maria looked at me strangely.

Met at the playground? MET AT THE PLAY-GROUND? Though, yeah. We probably *should* have. It would have been a lot less stress. But how was I supposed to know it would go so well?

I looked at my other friends, who I felt I'd let down. First there was Kristian. I was relieved he was safe and sound. *Not* eaten. But I'd had it with all of that!

Kristian said he was starting to feel a little dishonest about making a true-crime-style podcast when it wasn't actually true. And while I was really, really relieved about Bigfoot, I felt sort of bad. That podcast had taken a lot of work.

But Kristian had a solution.

I was really excited to be in this new version of the podcast. You know, now that I was an actor.

Well. As long as the friends don't actually *find* anything scary in the woods.

It seemed Rocco and Petra were okay, too.

I felt so relieved, Cosmo. About all of it. So relieved that I started giggling about hiding in the tree house and thinking I had to stay there for the rest of my life. That definitely wasn't how I planned today would go. Then again, this party, Chloe and Maria meeting—none of it was expected.

But maybe things don't always go as planned. And maybe, just maybe, that's okay.

THE NOISE

Dear Cosmo,

An hour later, the cast party was in full swing. We'd played Toss the Chicken, Freeze Tag, held a Hula-Hoop Contest, and came up with potential names for Mom's twins and Riley's mom's single baby.

TWIN NAMES
Itty and Bitty
Moon and Cloud
Elle and Emme
Ariel and Belle
Thor and Loki
Bonnie and Clyde
Kermit and Fozzie
Peppa and George

BABY NAMES
Finley
Jax
Morris
Marmaduke
Esmeralda
Gregory
Frieda
Cheeto

There was a moment when I considered telling Maria and Chloe what I'd overheard Riley tell Juice Box about feeling jealous of her mom's new baby . . . but then I reconsidered. After all, Riley hadn't told anyone that I'd ripped my dress on a nail so badly that my underwear was showing. So I decided to keep her secret, too.

After a while, people started to head home. Before she left, Miss Kettle passed around gifts for everyone in the play.

We all started laughing—even Miss Kettle. You know what's funny, Cosmo? I *like* Miss Kettle.

I mean, I'm never going to get used to her talking to Steve all day, but I like that Steve doesn't mess around. And she's a pretty fun teacher.

Then I saw Violet getting ready to leave. Before she took off, she pulled me aside.

That was a surprise. But as soon as Violet said it, I realized how much I'd wanted her to apologize.

The way we'd gone from best friends to . . . nothing. I hated thinking that she'd changed so much that she didn't even realize how hurt I'd felt.

But maybe she hadn't changed so much, after all.

I love my new friends, but I've missed Violet. And I've definitely learned something—just because I have new friends doesn't mean there isn't room for old ones. And just because I have lots of friends doesn't mean everyone has to hang out together . . . or even get along. But I have to let them decide that for themselves.

Well. Let's be real. I still wouldn't mind planning a few perfect picnics here and there.

Mrs. Hines left next.

I wanted to tell Mrs. Hines that I hadn't been excited about the play or anything. I mean, I'd held out until the very last minute, hoping that a plague of bugs would swarm the school and I wouldn't have to go on.

Then again, I *did* go on . . . and I didn't die!

So maybe I should take it as a win.

Not long after that, the only people left were my family and close friends—Maria, Chloe, Kristian, Rocco, and Petra. Since most of my friends hadn't seen my new room yet, I took them upstairs. All the adults and Juice Box and some of his buddies stayed downstairs, so it seemed like an adventure.

But as soon as I walked in, *this* happened.

Everyone said they heard it, too. That was good because at least I hadn't imagined it. It was also really scary ... because the screech was real.

Chloe was especially excited.

I was really hoping no one would take Chloe up on her suggestion.

And so, we crept into the hall. Then Kristian pointed to this thing in the ceiling that I hadn't noticed before.

Kristian explained that the little door led to the house's attic. I had no idea this house even *had* an attic. And what kind of weird house had a *door* in the ceiling? In my old house, the attic had stairs and a cute little room with a window seat.

Rocco stood on a box of books and pulled at the string hanging down from the door. And then *this* happened.

Okay. The ghost family *definitely* lived up there.

Rocco started to go up. Chloe followed him. Then they turned and looked at me. Everyone figured I was going to go up next. But I *couldn't*. It was just too scary.

Then I thought of something. I ran back into my room and grabbed Chloe's lucky rock. Sure, I'd been able to get through the school play without it, but ghosts were a whole different story.

I squeezed the rock in my hands. My heart started to slow. Clearly, there *was* something going on inside my house. And now we were going up to see what it was. But I was with my friends. I could do this.

We climbed up the stairs. It was dark. I was sure the attic was full of spiders and who knows what else. I wondered if we should be up here. What if that made the ghost family mad? What if it wasn't a ghost family at all but a giant rat . . . or a rabid raccoon . . . or something I hadn't even thought of?

The screech was even louder up here and much, *much* worse. But then Chloe turned on the flashlight on her phone . . . and we could see a little bit better.

He pointed to an old rusty ceiling fan. One of the blades was kind of bent, and it touched the ceiling. It seemed drafty up here, so whenever there was a little bit of wind, the fan moved . . . and the screech happened.

But that couldn't be right. Surely, the sound had to be something terrifying. A murderer living up here, maybe? Some sort of rabid troll? Where was the ghost family?

We searched the attic for anything else. There didn't seem to be any ghosts anywhere. Maybe it really *was* just a creaky old ceiling fan. Rocco used the handle of a broom to bend it back so it wasn't scraping anymore.

Just as we were about to go downstairs, though, Kristian called out.

The box looked old. Really old. But somehow, it didn't seem scary. More like . . . interesting. I wondered where it was from and who'd forgotten it here.

I cradled the box under my arm as I climbed back down the stairs. It wasn't very heavy, and it fit right on my hip. I really liked it, actually. It felt mysterious. I didn't even care if we couldn't figure out how to open it—I wanted to put it on my dresser as a decoration. It made me feel closer to this house. I wondered if this house had been waiting for someone to find this box for a long time . . . and now it was happy that I had.

Like Rocco says, houses have feelings, too.

EPILOGUE

Dear Cosmo,

Well, it's been three weeks since we moved into the house, and I have to say, it isn't as horrible as I thought. Our boxes are put away. The twins' room is done. So is the tree house. Dad finally caved and called a professional builder to make sure the thing wasn't going to totally collapse.

Took some HAMMERIN', but she's ALL SAFE now!

So, these days, I've been going into the tree house. It's nice up here. We've decorated it with twinkle lights and some beanbags. I've been asking my parents for a mini fridge, but so far they've said no. The only sad thing is that we haven't figured out a way to get you safely up here, Cosmo. I wish we could.

As for the box from the attic, we still haven't been able to find the key that goes with it. It's been fun hearing all my friends' guesses of what might be inside, though.

What if it's a box inside a box inside a box?

I bet it's a SECRET BOOK!

Maybe it's vintage roller coaster blueprints!

Or really cool old video games?

Or maybe something spooky! Like 20,000 PLASTIC EYEBALLS!

I have lots of guesses of what could be inside, too. In some ways, the idea that there could be *anything* inside the box is more fun than knowing what's actually in there.

I've been feeling pretty good now that the play is over, and now that Maria and Chloe have remet. I still feel a little silly I worried about this for so long. But in my defense, you hear something like "sworn enemies" . . . and what are you supposed to expect? Anyone would jump to conclusions!

Chloe sort of realized her mistake, I think.

I couldn't believe it. Could Chloe really not tell how much I worried? I've come to think that my worrying is as obvious as my hair color or the fact that I like to wear stripes. Remember in the fall, when Violet told me that I worry too much? I thought because she could tell I was panicking, *everyone* could. I thought it was so . . . obvious.

But maybe everyone has stuff that we can't immediately see. Stuff they worry about. Stuff that bugs them. Even Miss Kettle. Even Riley!

Anyway, as of this morning, there is something NEW to worry about. My mom walked into the kitchen with this nervous look on her face.

Time? Time for what? I looked at my dad. He was holding a suitcase. Were we going on a trip?

Then I realized. I'd *packed* my mom that suit-case. For the *hospital*.

It was time for . . . *that*?

I looked at Juice Box. He looked scared sud-denly, so I took his hand. There was a huge part of me that didn't want anything to change, either. But it was going to change whether we wanted it to or not, so I guess we'd better be ready. And then I thought one more time about that diving board Miss Hines kept talking about.

How was I supposed to dive into those guys? And why was the fly so *huge*?

But then I imagined myself in my bat costume from the play. I'm not sure why. Maybe because I'd felt so scared when I first put it on . . . but then I'd felt brave. I saw myself on that diving board with my bat wings. And then something happened in my mind. I imagined something new.

Mom's heading off to the hospital now, Cosmo! And Grandma Mimi, Juice Box, and I are going to hang out here and wait for news. It's going to be a wild ride . . . but I think I can get through it. I'm just glad I have you by my side.

ACKNOWLEDGMENTS

Once again, it has been a wonderful experience to continue the Penny journey. I want to thank those who have continued to champion all of her worries and adventures—the Alloy team of Lanie Davis, Sara Shandler, Josh Bank, Les Morgenstein, and Romy Golan, and everyone at Penguin Random House: Jen Klonsky, Matt Phipps, Marikka Tamura, and Suki Boynton; Anne Heausler, Bethany Bryan, Cindy Howle, and Rob Farren in proofreading and copyediting; and Diane McKiernan in Penguin Random House Audio—I can't wait to hear Penny as an audiobook! And let's not forget Jordana Kulak, Christina Colangelo, Amber Reichert, and Lauren Festa in marketing—thank you for all you're doing for Penny behind the scenes! (And thank you for enduring my many ideas of how we can get Penny out into the world.) Thanks also to Tom Lassally and Richard Abate at 3 Arts for your continuing support.

Big thanks to Jenny Marsh for reading *Penny Draws a Best Friend* to the third-grade class at Markham Elementary as some of her earliest readers, as well as Jaclyn Fulton, our school librarian—and all school librarians!—for encouraging the love of reading and getting great books into the right hands. A big hug to Kristian and Henry, as usual, for making guitars out of doorways and for writing comics about a super cactus—I can so see the two of you making the movie version of Petra's play, except maybe with weird stuffed animals. And finally, much love to Michael, who played not only a passerby but *also* the turkey in the school play. I'm sure it was just as impressive as Penny's performance, and the turkey costume must have been adorable.

Penny's story continues in

A SECRET ADVENTURE

Turn the page for a sneak peek!

PENNY DRAWS A SECRET ADVENTURE

Dear Cosmo,

I'm sure you know what's new—you can tell by all the strange smells and sounds. That's right, the twins are home.

Not all of us are excited about that.

I think my new baby brother and sister are kind of cute—even though they cry a lot. My parents are really trying to get Juice Box to come around.

That's one of Juice Box's favorite monster trucks. My parents said a baby can't be named The Disaster on Wheels. Juice Box had other suggestions handy: "What about Flame Thrower, Destructionator, or Big Buckaroo?"

My parents said I could help with names, too, but the problem is, Juice Box and I just can't agree on anything. But we'll keep trying!

Speaking of the babies, I kind of didn't realize how . . . *helpless* babies are. They can't do *anything*! They can't even hold up their heads! And my parents seem *far* too relaxed about all of it. I really think they need to reread this *Baby 101* book I found on a high shelf of the bookcase. They told me they had everything under control . . . but according to the book, I wasn't so sure.

The next morning, I couldn't find that baby book anywhere. I don't know what *that* was all about.

Because Mom and Dad have been so busy

with the babies, they've had people come over to make sure Juice Box and I eat nutritious dinners and don't set the house on fire. Sometimes it's Grandma Mimi or Grandma Anne. Other times it's this new babysitter from down the street. Her name is Grace.

Honestly? I think we'd be better off babysitting ourselves.

Good thing I have my friends to distract me from all the stuff happening at home. Kristian decided he needed new podcasting equipment for next season, so he started a dog-walking business to raise some money. We've had a nice time meeting other doggies, haven't we, Cosmo?

And Chloe and I have been exploring the neighborhood more. There's one house I won't even walk by ever again, though.

But the most exciting thing that happened was that my friends and I found the key to the mysterious box in the attic. It took forever to find! We made a big deal of opening it.

What did we find inside? Well, it's something that will send us on a secret adventure . . . one that's really exciting but also kind of scary. And I have a feeling I'm going to have tons of worries along the way.

So cross all your paws for me, Cosmo! With everything happening, I'm about to go on a very wild ride!

ABOUT THE AUTHOR

SARA SHEPARD is the author of the #1 *New York Times* bestselling series Pretty Little Liars, along with many other novels for young adults and adults. The Penny Draws series is her first one for younger readers. She lives in Pennsylvania with her husband, dogs, and sons Henry (who would have been named Penelope James had he been born a girl) and Kristian (who, like the character, loves all things roller coasters, especially riding them and talking about them).

31901069631184